For Julia with all my love

Snowy Valentine
Copyright © 2011 by David Petersen

Library of Congress Cataloging-in-Publication Data

Petersen, David, date

Snowy Valentine / written and illustrated by David Petersen. — 1st ed.

p. cm.

Summary: Jasper Bunny spends a snowy Valentine's Day visiting his forest friends in hopes of finding the perfect gift for his beloved Lilly.

ISBN 978-0-06-146378-5 (trade bdg.) — ISBN 978-0-06-146380-8 (lib. bdg.)

[1. Valentine's Day—Fiction. 2. Rabbits—Fiction. 3. Forest animals—Fiction. 4. Love—Fiction.] I. Title.

PZ7.P44188Sno 2011   2009027197

[E]—dc22   CIP

                                                                                                                    AC

Typography by Jeanne L. Hogle
12 13 14 15   LPR   10 9 8 7 6 5 4 3 2

SNOWY VALENTINE

Written and illustrated by David Petersen

HARPER

An Imprint of HarperCollinsPublishers

On a snowy Valentine's Day, Jasper Bunny still could not think of a gift good enough for Lilly. Jasper loved his wife very much. So he couldn't give her just any old gift.

"Perhaps seeing what my neighbors are doing for Valentine's Day will give me an idea for the perfect present," he thought.

He stopped at the Porcupines' house. "We are each knitting
a scarf for Mother," said the seven porcupine children.

A handmade scarf did seem like a good gift for Lilly, but Jasper couldn't get the hang of knitting.

On his way, Jasper saw a glow coming from the Frogs' window. "I bet Miriam will have a good suggestion," thought Jasper. "She always has such wonderful taste."

Inside, Miriam showed Jasper a box full of chocolate-covered flies. "Landon will be so excited when he wakes up!" she whispered.

"I'm sure he will," Jasper agreed pleasantly.

He thought, "This is a treat for a frog—but it's definitely not something my Lilly would enjoy!"

Still no gift in sight or mind, Jasper plodded past
Everett's wagon. "Step right up!" gushed the salesman.
"I've got beautiful blooms and fantastic flowers!"

But all of the raccoon's flowers had wilted from the cold.
None of them matched the beauty Jasper had in mind for Lilly.

Jasper was worried. It was getting late, and he still had nothing for Lilly.

"Jasper!" called Teagan. "What are you doing out on this cold, snowy Valentine's Day?"

"I'm searching for a gift for Lilly," Jasper replied, "but I don't know what to do."

"Come in and we'll brainstorm by the fire," Teagan said warmly.

"I do understand," Teagan said.

"I myself have been hunting all day for a Valentine's gift to impress my vixen, Faith. And I think *rabbit stew* is just the ticket!"
Before Jasper knew it, he was in the soup!

Terrified, Jasper waited for his chance. When Teagan walked away to pull out Faith's chair, Jasper sprang out of the pot and escaped, quick as a bunny.

Jasper was wet and cold and ready to give up when Spalding
called down. "This necklace of winter berries will make a
wonderful Valentine's gift for my mate, don't you think, Jasper?"

"Yes, it is a splendid gift," said Jasper sadly. "But I have nothing for Lilly. I have been around the entire valley, and I can't give her a handmade scarf or wilted flowers or chocolate flies or any gift at all if I become rabbit stew!"

The cardinal looked thoughtful. "Hmm . . . no gift, you say?
From where I sit, I see you have given Lilly a wonderful gift already."

Back at the burrow, Lilly stepped outside to wait
for Jasper. She saw the heart he had made for her . . .

. . . and she loved it.

Jasper's journey showed the greatest gift he could give:

his love for her.